DEAREST MALACHI KEOGH

N.R. WALKER

COPYRIGHT

Cover Artist: N.R. Walker
Editor: Boho Edits
Publisher: BlueHeart Press
Dearest Malachi Keogh © 2021 N.R. Walker
Dearest Milton James © 2021 N.R. Walker

BLURB

Julian Pollard never believed in love at first sight. That was until he met Malachi Keogh. Well, maybe it wasn't love at first sight, but it sure was something.

Julian had forgotten how to live, how to be happy, and Malachi changed all that. Now together for four years, Julian wants to give Malachi a Christmas he'll never forget.

The only problem is, Christmas at a mail distribution centre is the busiest time of the year. It just might take the whole team to make it happen.

Dearest Malachi Keogh

N.R. WALKER

CHAPTER ONE

I DIDN'T BELIEVE in love at first sight. I thought it was a preposterous notion for fools and people who didn't know any better. How could anyone have something shift inside them the second they meet someone?

Well, I'll tell you.

After years of heartbreak and loneliness, of closing myself off from the world around me, a bright ray of sunshine with a streak of blue in his hair that matched his neon boots, walked into my office and changed my life.

I didn't know how important he would become to me in that moment, but I knew he was . . . something.

He sure was something.

I tried to distance myself. I tried to tell myself he could never want someone like me, that it was foolish to think he would. Not to mention the whole work complication . . .

But my heart wouldn't be swayed.

We just had this instantaneous connection. Something I'd never experienced before. I stopped trying to fight it, and it turned into the best thing to ever happen to me.

Malachi fit into my life in every way.

He fit in my life like a piece I didn't even know was missing—with my family, with my friends, with me.

He didn't just fit in with everyone at work either. He joined our little eclectic patchwork of people and somehow made us better. We'd always been a friendly unit, but in the last four years, owing to Malachi's insistence, we became more of a team.

He just brightened up every room he walked into.

A knock at my office door snapped my attention. Cherry poked her head in. "You wanted to see me?"

Oh, shoot.

I'd been daydreaming again. Daydreaming about Malachi again.

"Yes, please come in. I know you're run off your feet. Is, ah . . ." I made a face. "Is Malachi still busy?"

She came in and sat in one of the two chairs opposite me at my desk. "Uh, yeah. You do know he's putting up more Christmas decorations?"

"Yeah, he asked me. I said it was fine."

"He's up a ladder draping tinsel and baubles from every surface. I think it's going to be worse than last year."

"He buys all the decorations really cheap after Christmas every year," I explained. "So there is more this year, so it *is* technically worse. And . . ." I cleared my throat. "My mother gave him all that stuff he's putting up today. I tried to stop them, but when they get together . . . I'd have more luck stopping the sun rise, to be frank. Honestly, I'd rather all the decorations be here than at home." Although he'd outdone himself there as well.

"It looks like Santa's Workshop exploded out there. And there were no survivors."

I smiled. "I'm sure it does."

"And Malachi told Paul he has a sexy elf costume for him to wear. What even is a sexy elf costume?"

"I don't think I want to know."

"Personally, I think Paul would be better suited as a reindeer, and the sexy elf should be left to Malachi."

I smiled. "Please do not suggest that."

Although, the mental imagery of him wearing something like that wasn't exactly unpleasant.

"I think Denise already did, so . . ." Cherry shrugged. "Too late." Then she paused for a second. "Um, you wanted to see me?"

"Yes! Yes, I do. It's a personal thing."

She looked horrified. "If it involves him wearing a sexy elf costume—"

"No, not that personal," I amended quickly. "It's not like that, it's just not exactly work-related."

Cherry frowned. "Oh, okay."

"And you can't tell Malachi about it."

She eyed me cautiously. "He's like a little ferret, you know that, right? Cute as hell, but sneaky too, and if he gets a sniff of something suspicious, he won't stop until he finds it."

I grinned at her. "Yes, I know. But it's his Christmas present."

"Oh."

"I need help making it happen."

She stared at me. "How?"

I felt stupidly giddy. Nervous and slightly nauseous. Taking a deep breath, I opened my top desk drawer, pulled out an envelope, and carefully placed it on the desk between us.

There was no address, no stamp. Just a name.

Dearest Malachi Keogh

"I'm going to ask him to marry me."

CHAPTER TWO

———

I'D WANTED to ask him for a long time.

And it had to be special. *He* was special. He was also fun and outlandish and far from clichéd. If anyone was deserving of a personal grand gesture that was anything but clichéd, it was Malachi.

Asking for help from Cherry was my best shot at making this happen. She knew him well, they'd become close, so between us we had a pretty solid scope on his thought process and how he might try and solve the mystery. But she was also very good at clues, and if he needed steering in any particular direction, she could do that without him becoming suspicious.

"This is going to take all of us," Cherry said. "To some degree. Even if it's just running interference or sending him on a wild goose chase to distract him."

I conceded a nod. "But can they keep it a secret?"

Her eyes narrowed. "They wouldn't dare spoil it."

Actually, she looked a little scary and I knew then why she and Malachi were such good friends.

"Excellent."

So we concocted a plan.

Well, I had a Plan A and Cherry helped me fine tune it. It probably wasn't foolproof and there was no contingency. If it fell apart at any time, I'd implement Plan B. Which was to forget trying to make it fun and just get down on bended knee and ask him outright.

But Plan A: Christmas was in seven days, there were five days of 'surprises' for Malachi which meant I had two days to put the first plan into action, and there were some details to perfect beforehand. And we were so busy at work that I'd spent most of my December on the floor running cages as well. Christmas was always the busiest time of the year; our workload easily tripled.

But I was using the fact Malachi was so busy to help make my plan work. Hiding stuff and keeping secrets from someone I lived with *and* worked with wasn't easy. And it would most likely take the whole team at work to make it happen.

So two days later, five days before Christmas, I gave Denise the first letter.

"Please put this on Malachi's cart. On top where it's not obvious but it can't get lost," I said, handing it over. "He can't know it came from me."

Denise nodded, her mission understood, and she took the envelope. "Is this it?"

"Yes."

"I'm on it," she said, determined.

It was heavy and thick for a letter. The paper and envelope were expensive and high quality. I'd been practising calligraphy, and while I was nowhere near good, it certainly didn't look like my normal handwriting. I'd even chosen the postage stamp just for this. The label on the front had gotten 'water damage' which was really Cherry using paper towel just damp enough to make it unreadable.

Paul had a postmark stamper, with the date and location, the kind that post offices used. I didn't ask where he got it from. I didn't want to know. But he'd very skilfully stamped the top corner so we could see it had been "processed." We just couldn't read any details.

Paul was very good at it. Probably too good at it, but I could hardly ask questions when he was doing me a favour. We had exactly ten seconds to get it done, and we were trying to keep it a secret from Malachi.

As it was, Malachi had spotted Paul leaving my office. It was a close call. But Paul had grinned, clapped his hands together. "Thanks for approving the use of the collection of mannequins and spare body parts in the storage room as a Christmas nativity scene."

Malachi went pale and wide-eyed, and he needed to sit down. "No, no no no no. No mannequins, no body parts." He put his hand to his forehead. "I feel ill. Julian, how could you do this to me?"

I was standing in my doorway, not sure how I was in trouble for any of this. Paul just smirked as he pushed his cart down aisle F-G. But it worked, because Malachi was so derailed by the mere horrific mention of a mannequin and fake body display, he'd forgotten all about Paul coming out of my office.

Malachi and Paul had an unusual relationship. They joked with one another all the time and they were mostly friendly, though sometimes the barbs were a little sharp. But they each gave as good as they got, and I think they both liked pushing each other's buttons every so often.

"There will be no spare body parts as a nativity scene," I said, patting Malachi's shoulder as I walked past. On my way to collect a full cart of parcels and letters, I smiled when I saw Malachi's cart with tinsel draped along the outside.

His letter was sitting on top, near the side, with all the other envelopes. Not super obvious, but the sight of it made my belly all tight with knots.

I began processing my cart while keeping one eye on Malachi and where he was and if he'd got to the letter yet, all without trying to be too obvious.

I was just about done with my first cart when Theo pushed his cart past me. "He's reading it," he whispered as he went by.

With my heart in my throat, I pushed my cart back up the long aisle toward the front. I stopped a fair distance from the end, but I could see Malachi sitting at his desk in his cubicle. He was holding the letter in one hand, his other hand pressed to his heart. His eyes were wide and, oh god, was he teary?

My heart banged against my ribs, trying to escape out my mouth. I felt a little queasy.

Then Malachi hugged the letter, and I must have laughed or made some kind of thankful/relieved sound because Malachi spun to look at me.

Shit.

"What are you doing?" I asked, trying to cover up why I was watching him. "Do you hug all the mail?"

He stood up and held out the letter. "Julian . . . Julian, come and read this," he said.

I walked toward him, my chest tight. I tried to smile. "What is it?"

"You have to read this. No, let me read it to you." He sat back down, patted down his hair, and let out a long breath. "It's beautiful."

My heart stammered in my chest. "So read it."

Malachi shook himself and inhaled deeply. "Okay, are you ready?"

"Yes."

"It reminds me of the Dearest Milton James letters."

I almost laughed. "Okay."

He let out a slow breath. "There's no name, but it's written in calligraphy. The ink is a pretty blue." He made a face. "It's not as neat as the Milton James letters though."

I tried not to be offended. "Fair enough."

"But it's a valiant attempt."

"I'm sure it is," I said. "Malachi, please."

"Right. Okay." He took another breath in and began to read.

"Merry Christmas, my love. I wish I could give you the world, for it feels like that's what you've gifted me. A love so pure, so complete. I wish for nothing when I'm with you.

May this Christmas bring you all you could ask for, may all your wishes come true.

Forever yours."

Malachi stood up and turned the paper around so I could see the writing. "Isn't it just the most precious thing ever?"

"It's very sweet," I whispered, not trusting my voice for much more.

"I need to find who sent it," he declared, turning back to his desk. "I have to. So we can find who they sent it to. They need to get this before Christmas."

I tried not to smile. "Okay."

He sat down and pulled the envelope over, inspecting it with his nose almost touching it. "I might have to stay late," he said, still studying the envelope.

I worried for a second that he might see something we'd missed. "Okay."

He shot me a look. "It's very important, Julian," he said, annoyed now. "Someone has gone to the trouble of writing this beautiful letter for Christmas and it's been ruined. I have to find them."

I smiled at him then. "Okay."

He sat upright. "I need a black light. Paul has one. I think he uses it to search hotel rooms for fun." He stood up. "Paul?" he called out, taking both the letter and the envelope with him as he went down aisle J-K. "Paul, I need your creepy torch."

He disappeared and I turned back to find Cherry watching me.

"No, you're not putting fentanyl on it," Malachi said from somewhere down a far aisle.

Cherry smiled and I grinned. The first letter was done.

Four days, four letters to go.

CHAPTER THREE

"THERE'S NOTHING," Malachi mumbled, his forehead pressed to his desk. "I can't find anything. The address is completely water damaged. The postmark isn't legible at all."

"It's how it goes sometimes," I offered gently.

Everyone had left twenty minutes ago; the night shift was arriving but giving us a wide berth. Malachi's pitiful whining was worthy of an Oscar.

I had to wonder how he'd handle the next four letters. Probably not very well.

He looked up at me. "Who writes this kind of love letter without a return address? Do they not care? How can they put such thought and effort into the purchase of the expensive paper, the ink, to sit and write such beautiful words from the heart, then take the time to post it and not write a bloody return address? Who does that?"

I sighed. "Someone who thought—"

"An idiot," he said sharply. "That's who."

I held out my hand. "Come on. Let's go home."

He pouted, cutely, of course, and reluctantly took my hand. "I'm going to need carbs to get through this."

I pulled him to his feet. "Carbs for dinner it is then."

"And also carbs for dessert."

I laughed. "For you. I look at food and gain weight. You can eat all the carbs you want, apparently. I don't fancy two hours on the dreadmill to work it off."

He always laughed when I called it that. Now he smiled, not a laugh, but at least it was better than his pouty frown. "You can spend two hours working me over if you'd prefer."

"I would prefer that, very much."

He sighed, still smiling. "Well, my day just improved exponentially."

He was such a brat. And yes, even at thirty-one years of age, Malachi could still be a brat, and I would hope he'd still be one in his eighties. Nothing would make me happier if he was old and grey, still wearing funky-coloured boots and a matching Hello Kitty or Miss Sunshine shirt, with his quick wit, sassy mouth and wicked sense of humour.

He was a brat in the bedroom too. Always mouthing off until he got what he wanted. And what he wanted was to be face down on the bed, sprawled out and spread wide, and drilled into the mattress.

I hardly minded giving it to him.

When we got home, I unlocked the front door and held it open for him. It was hot and humid, typical Sydney weather in December. I set the air conditioning going while Malachi scooped up Mr Bojangles and gave him a quick cuddle. Mr Bojangles was a gift from me to Malachi when he moved in with me and missed Buster Jones, his old neighbour's cat.

Mr Bojangles was a rescue cat and Malachi adored

him. I gave the cat a quick pat, then kissed Malachi. "Why don't you go run a bath, and I'll start dinner," I suggested.

Malachi hummed and sighed happily. "Have I ever told you how much I love that you look after me?"

"Yes, you have," I replied, kissing him again. "But you can tell me again."

"I love you, Julian." He leaned up on his toes and kissed me. "I love how you look after me, and I really love how you're going to fuck me for two hours later."

I scoffed. "I think your expectations far exceed my capabilities."

"Oh, I don't think so. I want to fall asleep a sweaty mess, unable to move, unable to think, and I know you know how to do that." He smirked over his shoulder as he headed up the stairs before he coddled Mr Bojangles. "Daddy knows what I need, doesn't he?"

I smiled watching him disappear upstairs. Yes, I knew what he needed and I knew exactly how to give it to him. And knowing he would be in the bathroom making himself ready made my body thrill at what was coming.

By the time I served dinner, I was already half-hard in anticipation. It didn't help that he was wearing only a black silk robe, smelling fresh, his black hair damp and brushed back.

I missed the flair of colour he used to wear in his hair. That streak of blue or purple or bright red that he'd match with his outfits. He stopped dyeing it before his 30th birthday, saying he was too old to act so young.

I understood. I just missed it.

I liked running my hand through Neon Purple strands, or Solar Orange, Teal Teaser. It was too easy to fist a handful of it when I was fucking him from behind.

"Julian?" Malachi was looking at me, his head tilted. "You okay?"

I realised then I'd been so lost in my thoughts, my fork still in my hand. "Yes. I'm fine."

His smile turned smug. "You thinking about anything in particular? Because you have a look in your eyes that I rarely see outside of the bedroom."

I growled and pushed my plate away. I met his gaze and licked my lips. "I'm thinking about being buried inside you and the look in your eyes when I fill you with come."

Malachi blinked and swallowed hard, his lips parted, licked-wet. His chest heaved and he gently laid his fork down. Then he stood up, letting his robe fall open, revealing his very naked body underneath. "Where do you want me?" he asked, his voice just a whisper. "Bent over the couch or in bed?"

I was fully hard now. My cock was uncomfortably confined in my trousers, and the couch was closer . . . but the bed was more comfortable for him.

"Bed."

He whimpered as he turned and made his way up the stairs. I took a second to control myself before I followed him up. When I walked into our room, he was bent over the edge of the bed, a towel over the covers, with his robe pulled up, reaching around to rub lube over his hole.

Fuck.

I took his wrist and brought his hand up over his head, leaning over him, pressing my hips against him, letting him feel how turned on I was.

"That's my job," I whispered into the back of his head. "I take care of you." He whined and I kissed the nape of his neck. I ran my hands down his ribs, to the small of his back, then over the curve of his arse. I took over, lubing him up and gently stretching him with my fingers until he was writhing and mumbling impatient complaints.

So I popped the button on my trousers and unzipped the fly. I pulled my cock out and applied a stream of lube before pushing the cockhead against his entrance.

He gripped the covers, readying himself, lifting his hips a little, waiting . . .

I pushed into him, his tight warmth drawing me in. He threw his head back and groaned through the breach.

He was used to me now. He could take me like a champ, and he loved it. He craved it. And I loved giving it to him.

We'd long forgone the use of condoms and it had taken our sex life to a whole new level. I'd never gone raw with anyone before him, and he'd never received it before me.

There was no feeling like it, and knowing he took my seed made it hotter, made it better. There was something primal in me, marking him like that, that I got off on.

He belonged to me.

Or it made me belong to him, I wasn't sure.

Both.

"Fuck, Julian, yes," he breathed as I pulled back and pushed in, deeper, all the way.

I gripped his hips and leaned forward, knowing by his reaction that I was now pressing in at a different angle. His knuckles were white as he fisted the bed covers, as he arched his back. Letting go of his hips, I wrapped my arms around his chest and lifted him upright. His knees found the mattress to take his weight, but he was impaled on me. He groaned, almost a wail, before he stroked himself.

"Malachi," I grunted, not sure how long I could hold out for.

He was too hot, too tight, too much.

He lurched forward, his whole body jerking as he cried

out, coming onto the towel. So I drilled into him, prolonging his orgasm and speeding toward my own.

When he cried out the final time, his body going slack on the bed, I held his hips, and with a last thrust, I came inside him.

He whined as he took it, feeling every pulse, every drop. It was this hot, this perfect, every time.

I wanted to stay inside him forever. I wanted to be one with him, this deep, this complete for the rest of my life.

I pushed him further up the mattress and pressed my weight onto him as I lay down. We caught our breath, and when I began to pull out of him, his hand on my hip stopped me.

"Stay."

"Mm." I kissed his shoulder, his nape, the shell of his ear. "You want more?"

He smiled before pressing his face into the bed covers, and he rolled his hips a little.

Christ.

It didn't take much, considering I was still buried inside him. Any sensitivity soon became pleasure, and gentle rolls of my hips became thrusts. Knowing I was fucking my come further into him made me push even deeper.

I gave him a second load, and because I came before him, I rolled him over and manoeuvred his legs so I was between them. I took his cock into my mouth and made short work of him that way.

He tasted sublime.

Malachi fell asleep, extremely sated and thoroughly had. He could barely string a sentence together, so the odds of him giving the letter at work another thought were nil.

Until he got the next one, that is.

CHAPTER FOUR

THE SECOND LETTER was going to come down to Theo's acting ability, and to be honest, I had my doubts. But his usual naivety would hopefully work in my favour because Malachi would be sceptical that Theo could be part of any conspiracy.

Just after lunch, Theo came out holding the opened letter. "Uh, hey, Malachi?" he called out.

Malachi was three aisles over. He left his cart and poked his head out. "Yeah, what's up?"

Theo held up the letter. "I think I have another letter . . ."

Malachi's eyes were already trained on the expensive paper and familiar blue calligraphy. "Oh my god! Did that come today?"

"Uh, yeah. It was in my cart. I was just processing—"

Malachi took it and gasped, his eyes wide. I was working with my own cart, trying not to seem obvious. "What is it?"

He spun around to me. "Look! It's another letter!" Theo

handed over the envelope it came in and Malachi ran to his desk.

Theo winked at me and went back to pushing his cart, and I finished processing a few parcels, giving Malachi enough time to sit down and read it.

I eventually followed him and found him tapping away at his keyboard. "What did you find?"

He was so excited he almost bounced off his chair. He picked up the letter to show me. "Look, Julian. It's the same."

I ignored the letter and picked up the envelope instead. "Water damage again."

"Yep. How is that possible? Is the postman sabotaging the mail deliberately? Is this person putting the letters in an old red box that's full of water?"

I shrugged. "There's been storms most afternoons this week."

"Yes, but why this person's mail? Why not everyone's mail?"

Cherry held up a parcel with obvious water damage. "This is the third one today."

He sighed and sagged, still holding the letter. "The entire postal system needs better safeguards in place to prevent this from happening."

Jeez. Before he could call his father and demand a national overhaul of the entire postal service, I gave his shoulder a squeeze. "Read me the letter."

He sighed again but sat up straight and composed himself.

"Merry Christmas, my love."

He looked up at me. "Everything after that is moot. That's possibly the best salutation I've ever read."

I smiled at him, barely refraining myself from taking his face, kissing him in front of everyone, and whispering 'Merry Christmas, my love' to him.

Barely.

He began the letter again.

"Merry Christmas, my love,

I will never take for granted waking up next to you every day. No day truly begins until I see you smile.

Your eyes give me butterflies, your laughter fills me with hope. These little gifts you give without a word.

I am, every day, thankful for you."

Malachi sighed when he put the letter down. "It's so romantic I think I might die."

"Well, please don't," I said. "I'd prefer it very much if you didn't do that."

He rolled his eyes and frowned at the letter. "I need to find this person. I need to see these letters delivered before Christmas."

I offered him a sad smile. "All you can do is try."

"Not try, Julian. I must. Whoever this person is writing to needs to know."

"Well, don't forget the rest of the cages," Denise said as she walked past on her way into the breakroom. "There's a lot to get through today."

He glowered at her, somewhat resembling an angry Muppet. It was cute.

I picked up the envelope again. "Where are you going to start looking? You have limited time right now."

Malachi pointed to his computer screen. "I was going to look at the weather patterns to see if I can determine which areas have been the wettest. But it could have been posted from Byron Bay and got wet in transport. I can thank the quality of the envelope for the fact the letter's not damaged. So that's one good thing, I guess."

I handed him the envelope. "If it were me, I'd start with the paper. It's expensive. Surely there aren't many places in Australia that sell it."

"I looked yesterday," he said glumly.

The truth was he'd be very unlikely to find any places in Australia that sold it, considering I ordered it from Japan. It cost me a fortune. Not a small fortune either.

I'd practised my calligraphy every time he went out somewhere. Quite often I'd lined up for Moni to drag him to the thrift shops for hours at a time just so I could practice. Writing on that expensive paper for the first time was nerve-racking. I almost couldn't bring myself to do it.

"It is beautiful paper," Malachi murmured, studying the letter again. His tone was wistful but also resigned. The very last thing I wanted was for him to be sad about these letters.

I gave his shoulder another squeeze. "Well, good luck. If you need me, I'll be . . ." I gestured down the aisle where my cart was still waiting.

I left him to it, hoping he wouldn't get very far with the source of the paper. I mean, surely he wouldn't.

And he didn't. He tried a few different avenues that went nowhere before going back to the rest of the packages and parcels he had to sort, but that didn't mean he wouldn't spend all evening after dinner on his laptop at home trying various searches for different kinds of expensive paper.

"This looks similar," he said. He was looking so closely, his nose was basically pressed to the screen. He couldn't take the actual letters from work, but he'd taken a close-up photo of the paper for reference. He was now comparing it to samples he found online. "This detail . . . I think it's handcrafted. I had no idea expensive paper was so . . ." He looked over at me. "There is a whole industry for this. There is one place in Sydney that supplies this quality. I can call them tomorrow."

I stroked Mr Bojangles' head. He'd chosen my lap tonight because Malachi had his laptop in his. "Hopefully they can point you in the right direction," I said.

Hopefully they could not.

He put his laptop on the coffee table, scooped Mr Bojangles from me, laid down, and plonked his feet in my lap instead.

"You right now?"

Malachi grinned. "Much."

I took the hint and began to massage his foot, rubbing my thumb into the arch and making him groan. "Is there any part of my body you don't know how to play?"

"Play?"

"Like a piano."

I smiled. "I never was musically talented."

"I beg to differ."

I finished the first foot and started on his second. "Oh, Mum wants us to bring that avocado and sweet chilli salad for Christmas lunch."

"Mm," he groaned as I hit a certain spot under his toes. "My sweet chilli dressing brings all the mums to the yard."

I snorted. "Did you get the list of things your mum wanted?"

He scratched Mr Bojangles under the chin. "I'll go tomorrow after work. If you need anything, make me a list."

The cat stood up on his chest and jumped down, sauntering away. Malachi stood up and offered me his hand. "Come on, we're going to finish this full body massage in bed."

I went very willingly. "Your wish, my command."

THE THIRD LETTER WAS DIFFERENT. It was still technically paper, but the envelope was bigger and it was wrapped with wax paper for protection. This gift was delicate, and I only trusted Cherry with it. The plan was to give it to him with about an hour to go before we finished. That way he couldn't torture himself all day with it.

Malachi had made some phone calls earlier to the expensive paper suppliers. He'd sent close-up photos of the paper and the envelope, but he'd yet to hear back.

So he was busy with his non-stop supply of carts full of parcels and letters when a call came in from the paper supply store. He was so excited as he ran to his desk, his eyes wide, smiling and nodding as he listened, but it soon faded to disappointment. "Well, thank you anyway. I really appreciate it. I know you're busy."

He hung up the call and sighed, defeated. "Dammit."

"Is everything okay?" I asked. I had a stack of letters in my hand so I looked like I was busy and hadn't been spying on him.

"She said no to the paper. They don't stock it. She said

it looks Japanese. And very expensive. Like, *really* expensive."

Shit.

Well, she was right.

I frowned. "Oh. But the letters weren't sent from Japan."

He shook his head. "Nope. Australian postmark." He sighed again. "I think."

Cherry made a nervous face behind her cubicle wall, holding today's letter, and she stood up. "Malachi?" She handed it over. "Does this envelope look familiar? I think it's the same expensive paper as the others."

It was A4, so the size was different, yes. But the paper was unmistakably the same.

She then held up the card. "This was in it. I just got to it now. I haven't looked . . ."

Malachi jumped to his feet and took the card, his eyes wide. "The paper is the same," he whispered. He laid the card on his desk and gently opened it.

It was a fold-out pop-up multi-layered kirigami piece, Christmas themed, with gold and red trees and origami reindeer. It was the same paper as the other letters, of course, and on the background was big calligraphic writing.

Merry Christmas, my love.
Now and forever.

Malachi looked up at everyone, his expression shock and disbelief. "It's the same. It's the . . . how can it all be the same?" He shook his head. "Something's not right."

Shit.

"It was opened," Cherry said quickly. She then held up the envelope. "See? The seal was already unstuck. I don't know if anything fell out. Maybe yesterday's letter was also in this envelope, because you couldn't be sure if it was post-marked or not . . ."

Okay, that was good. Sewing the seed of disbelief, of a number of possibilities. Casting doubt over how these pieces came to be here, all undeliverable.

Malachi sat there, shaking his head. "Why would someone spend so much money on the paper—this card must have cost a fortune—only to not take care of the shipping? If it was that expensive, why weren't they courier-delivered or hand-delivered? If they had this kind of money, why didn't they hire someone in a suit and expensive car to personally deliver the letters?"

It hurt to see him so crestfallen. This was supposed to be fun and exciting, not make him sad.

"Maybe the person who sent them is old-fashioned," I offered with a shrug. "Maybe the person who was supposed to receive them loved getting mail."

He looked at me for a long moment before conceding a nod. "Maybe."

"We don't know anything about them," I said.

He shook his head again, resigned this time. "There are no clues, no hints, no information outside of the fact that the person who sent them is the most romantic person ever and the person who was supposed to receive them won't get them. Not before Christmas, maybe not ever. And that's so sad. It's two days before Christmas. Tomorrow is Christmas Eve and we don't work Christmas Day, so tomorrow is my last chance to find them. They should have got the best Christmas present ever, and now we can't deliver it." He scowled at his computer screen for a second, then obviously had a bright idea because he turned to me, excited again. "Can I call the TV stations? Can I make these public? I'm certain they'd eat up such a feel-good Christmas story right now."

"Do you know how many crack-pots would come forward?" Paul asked from his cubicle. He didn't stand up or anything. "You'd be burying yourself in a few thousand dead ends and countless wasted hours."

Denise came out of the breakroom and cracked a can of Coke. "Every other parcel and envelope that you're ignoring in your cage right now is just as important. Hate to be the bringer of truth and facts, but . . ." She shrugged.

Malachi stared at her, and I felt bad. She was right, and I'd increased everyone's workload at the busiest time of the year.

"You're right," Malachi mumbled. He got to his feet. "I should get back to it."

"Malachi," I began, "I think we should talk—"

Cherry jumped up and grabbed Malachi's arm. "You can talk at home," she said. "We have mail to sort." She gave me a pointed glare as she dragged him toward his abandoned cart. "Come on, I'll help you."

I watched them disappear down an aisle and sighed. Denise was suddenly beside me. "I didn't really mean that. It was just a distraction. I mean, the other mail is important, but I could see you teetering on the brink of collapse there. You were about to tell him, so I had to say something."

Paul clapped my shoulder. "Hold your course, son. You're almost home and hosed. Just one more day to go."

I nodded but didn't really feel any better. "One more day."

"Tomorrow's the big one," Theo whispered.

Yes, it was.

"Oh, don't forget to dress up," Denise added. "Got your costume's ready?"

I'd almost forgotten about that. "Malachi's been planning mine for six months, so yes."

Then a high-pitched scream cut the air. We all spun to the sound. There was only one person who could scream that high.

"Malachi." I ran down the aisle, everyone else right behind me, to find Malachi backed against a shelf and Cherry peering into an open box on the ground.

Malachi was pale, his hand to his heart. Cherry reached into the box and pulled out a hand. A mannequin's hand, no less. And then another.

As it turned out, it was a box full of hands.

Malachi made a sound that was half gag, half whimper, and he shuddered from head to foot. Instinctively I went to him, pulling him against me. "It's okay."

He let out a heaving breath. "Who would do that? Who would send that?" He looked up at me with those big blue eyes. "What kind of person would order a box of hands? What kind of monster does that?"

"Well, I think *monster* is a bit harsh—"

"Monster, Julian."

Paul picked a hand out of the box, but I shot him a glare over the top of Malachi's head, silencing whatever he was about to say. It wouldn't have ended well. He smartly chose to drop the hand back into the box.

Malachi straightened up, patted down his shirt, then put his hand to his forehead. "I'm fine. It's fine. Sorry for the scream."

I checked my watch. It was ten minutes to five. "How about we call it a day?"

Everyone stood there staring at me for a silent beat, then shrugged. "Okay."

Paul picked the box up off the floor. "I'll put these in my cart for tomorrow," he said, disappearing down the aisle.

Cherry patted Malachi's arm before walking back to the front with Theo and Denise. "See you in the morning."

Malachi and I waited until we were alone. "You okay?" I asked.

He nodded. "Yeah. I don't know why it freaks me out so much. Sorry."

"Don't apologise." I cupped his face and kissed him softly. "Let's go home."

He sighed like that was the best thing he'd heard all day. We shut off our computers and packed up, saying our goodbyes as we walked out. Malachi was quiet in the car until he turned to me. "What do you think Paul is going to do with those hands?"

I laughed and took his hand. "He'll catalogue them and shelve them."

"He won't . . ." His eyes went wide. "Oh god. If he makes a Christmas tree out of those, he'll need a whole team of proctologists to have them removed."

I snorted. "He won't."

"Or Christmas tree ornaments. Lord. It would be in the *Guinness Book of Records* as the creepiest tree ever, and he'd be in every medical journal for having to have them surgically removed."

I laughed. "He wouldn't do that with inventoried mail." Then I shrugged. "He might buy his own, but he wouldn't take inventory."

He stared at me. "You're not helping."

"I'm joking." I lifted his hand to my lips. "Are you still going to the supermarket this afternoon?"

He sighed. "I forgot about that. I guess so, why?" He went from deflated to excited in half a second. "Do you have special Christmas gifts for me that you have to wrap and need me out of the house?"

I rolled my eyes. "No."

"You totally do." He did a little wiggle in his seat. "Then I shall totally give you all the time you need."

"Do you have gifts for me that need wrapping?" I asked.

"I wear underpants every day."

I laughed. "Your arse is a gift, that's very true."

He grinned. "You can unwrap it and play with it tonight, if you want. Santa might only come once a year, but you certainly don't need to. And you may think my arse is the gift, but honestly your dick and come inside me is the real gift."

God. He knew how to make my body react. Even after four years, he only had to talk about sex and my dick heard. I shifted in my seat. "I think we'll have to, yes."

He laughed, smug and proud. "Or I could forget the shopping and we could just fuck all evening."

That made me groan. "Malachi."

He sighed. "Okay, I'll behave. Unless you want to punish me . . ."

I chuckled. "It's not punishment when you beg for it."

He pouted, playful and cute, but the incident with the box of hands was forgotten, as were the expensive Christmas letters and Christmas card.

We got home and Malachi left almost straight away with his list of food and last-minute Christmas Day items to get. As soon as he was gone, I called my mum to say the coast was clear, then took out the few smaller things I'd bought for him and quickly wrapped them and put them under the tree.

A knock rapped on the front door, followed by a familiar sing-songed, "Julian?"

I opened the door and gave my mum a hug. "Come in."

"Is he here?"

"No. He has a few things to get, but you know he'll be looking at all the Christmas decorations until closing time."

Mum smiled. "Oh yes." She opened her huge handbag and took out an envelope. "Here's the last one."

My stomach tightened. "Thank you."

"It's no problem," she said, smiling sweetly. "The others have all gone according to plan?"

I nodded. "As much as they could. There was almost a meltdown today because he realised he has no way of delivering the letters to the poor person who was supposed to get them."

She frowned. "Oh dear."

"But he did say it was the most romantic thing he'd ever seen, so there's that."

"He doesn't suspect a thing?"

"Nope."

"Are you nervous?"

"Yes and no. Yes, because it's nerve-racking and this whole planning thing seemed like a good idea, but now it's drawn out and excruciating, and I probably should have just asked him outright months ago when I started all this." I shrugged. "And no, because I love him."

"And because you know he'll say yes because he loves you so much." Mum gave me a teary smile. "How about a cup of tea?"

"Good idea."

So we drank some tea, even though it was scorching hot outside, and we talked about everything we needed to bring and organise for Christmas lunch. Mum and Dad had hosted a fancy Christmas Day lunch for as long as I could remember. My whole family would be there. We'd eat far too much food and spend the afternoon laughing as we sipped on a glass of my dad's expensive Italian dessert wine.

The first Christmas Malachi and I spent together, he'd said Christmas lunch with my family was the best family thing he'd ever experienced. He couldn't remember anyone's names, but he adored them, and they adored him, of course.

We'd then spent Christmas dinner with his family, and it was a different feel. My family Christmas lunch was my parents and sisters and their kids, plus a dozen first and second cousins and their kids and all my aunts and uncles, and sometimes even the neighbours; it was far too crowded and loud, but wonderful in every way.

Malachi's family Christmas dinner was just his parents and his brother and sister and their kids. Still lovely, but rather formal and very polite. When he once said he was the rainbow sheep of his family, he wasn't kidding. I'm sure there would have been Freudian explanations as to why Malachi and I were both the odd sheep in our families, yet we'd fallen in love with someone who fit in with our own families better than we did.

Whatever the reason, it just worked.

They'd accepted me into their family with open arms, and if we'd ever thought his dad might have been mad about me and Malachi, it was the opposite. I think he considered me a good influence on Malachi, stable and settled.

Malachi *did* tell him it was just because I had a huge cock, but his dad told him to stop being crude. That was our second Christmas . . .

Anyway, the point was our families were great, and my mum was very excited about me asking Malachi to marry me. She was part of it, of course. I'd had to have the paper sent from Japan to her house so Malachi wouldn't find it.

"Oh, I think that's him now," Mum said.

Malachi came in through the back door, juggling bags in his arms, his phone still pressed to his ear. "Oh, I absolutely will," he said, putting his bags on the dining table. He was distracted and busy; I assumed he was talking to Moni. "No, I fully plan on having him rearrange my internal organs tonight—"

It was at that particular moment he noticed my mother sitting on the couch.

Oh, dear god.

He made a strange gurgling noise. "Moni, I have to go," he whispered, then ended the call. He stared at my mum. "Oh my goodness, I'm sorry you had to hear that. I was just—"

My mother waved him off. "Never mind, dear. Julian inherited his from his father, so I know all about having internal organs rearranged."

I gawped at my mother. "Mum!"

Malachi laughed. "Can I get you a drink? A donut cushion to sit on, perhaps?"

Mum laughed and I sighed.

I wasn't kidding when I said he fit in with my family.

CHAPTER FIVE

MALACHI WAS UP EARLY because it was Christmas costume day, and when I woke, my costume was laid out neatly on the bed for me.

He'd made us all do this every year since he started working with us. In the last four years, I'd gone as a gingerbread man and a reindeer—because 'it would be a shame not to use all that brown in my wardrobe'—a Santa Claus and a Christmas tree.

Yes, a tree, complete with baubles and tinsel.

If you knew Malachi, this would not surprise you. It did make for an interesting surprise visit by Malachi's father when all the staff were dressed as different types of Christmas characters.

He'd taken one look at me, dressed head to foot in green with baubles pinned and tinsel wrapped, complete with a hat with a star on top, and he stopped dead in his tracks and stared.

"Malachi?"

I'd nodded. He didn't really need to ask. Because there could only be one reason I was dressed like that.

But then Malachi had walked out dressed as an elf, complete with striped tights and curled elf shoes, with Cherry, who was the gothest Mrs Claus to ever exist, and Malachi's dad had simply nodded as if everything made perfect sense.

This year I was going as . . . Oh no. "Malachi, I am not wearing that."

He laughed as he walked out of the bathroom wearing a red sweater vest. "It'll be fun."

I stared at him. "And you probably shouldn't wear that."

"We'll be matchy-matchy," he said. "In funny Christmas sweaters."

"It's going to be forty degrees today," I said. "And . . . I am not wearing that."

The sweater he'd chosen for me had a knitted bauble on it with big writing that proudly read *Well Hung*, and Malachi's sweater vest read *Santa's Favourite Ho*.

I stared at him, horrified. "Malachi . . ."

He gestured to both sweaters. "Where is the lie? They're both accurate. I was going to get you the one that had *Snowballs Deep* on it and I could have gone as a snowball, but I thought you'd never go for that."

I laughed. "Well, no."

But then he grinned. "I'm just kidding. Your real costume is here," he said, walking into the walk-in wardrobe and coming out carrying a red suit. Not just any red suit, but a business suit made to look like Santa. "It's not heavy so you won't get too hot," he said.

I stared, for real this time. "I'm going as Santa?"

"Yes, you are. But a sexy-as-fuck Santa. Not the old podgy kind."

"Is there any such thing as a sexy Santa?" I asked.

Malachi nodded slowly. "Oh yes."

"And what are you going as?" I asked.

He pointed to his sweater vest. "I'm wearing this. You're Santa, and I'm your favourite ho." He stuck out a very naked leg. "I have stripy elf tights and hot pants and an elf hat with a bell."

I snorted. "Of course you do."

He handed me the suit, then took the sweater off the bed. "And just so you know, we're keeping this sweater for a winter costume party or something. Maybe you could wear it to my parents' place for Christmas dinner."

I snorted. "Or maybe I could not do that."

He clapped his hands. "Come on. Let's get dressed and ready. We have to take in the Kris Kringle gifts and the cupcakes. Don't let me forget."

Oh, yes. Cake had become a thing for every event, but at least this was just one cupcake each, with red or green frosting, instead of a whole cake.

Malachi wasn't kidding about the sexy Santa outfit. It was red, had a black belt, white cuffs, and of course, he'd gotten the boots to go with it. The suit was fitted, much tighter than necessary, much to Malachi's delight.

Aaaaand a fake beard. But oh no, not a long, white, fluffy Santa beard. This was fake, stick-on grey stubble that Malachi clearly liked. "That's hot."

"I look like a porno Santa," I complained.

Malachi's wide eyes matched his grin. "That's the look I was going for!"

I looked at myself side-on, seeing the curve of my arse, the skin-tight fabric stretched across my thighs. "It's bordering on obscene."

"It's bordering on hot as fuck," Malachi murmured.

I looked him up and down, with his striped tights and hot pants, his tight knitted red vest with *Santa's Favourite*

Ho on it, and his green elf hat. "If we get arrested for solici-
tation . . ." I grumbled. "And so God help me, if your father
turns up today."

Malachi preened a little, adjusting his hat. "He will
know, without a single doubt, who is responsible."

I sighed. At least this was a distraction for the final letter
he was to get today.

I groaned. "Let's get this over with."

Kris Kringle gifts and cupcakes in hand, we went to
work. Thankfully we were not pulled over by the police or
stuck in roadworks where someone could see us.

And it really was a Christmas miracle that we made it to
work before everyone else. At least we didn't have to make a
grand entrance looking like Santa Daddy and his Slutty Elf.

Cherry arrived next. She was a bonbon. Literally a giant
goth bonbon. She was in a huge cardboard tube, painted
black with different patterns, with gold ribbon at the top
and bottom. There were holes for her arms and face, of
course, but she looked great.

I had concerns about how she would sit down though.

It was a little odd that Denise wasn't in yet, given she
was usually in before me, unloading trucks and cages. But
then we heard laughter coming from the aisles and out
walked the Virgin Mary and her donkey.

Well, it was actually Denise as Mary in her blue biblical
outfit. Theo and Paul were the donkey. You know the kind
where one is the front and one is the arse in a horse suit?
Well, Paul was the head, Theo was the backend.

Denise was leading the donkey with a bridle from
Paul's mouth. I certainly wasn't game to ask why it
appeared to fit as though it was personally made for him.

Malachi laughed so hard he pulled a muscle in his side,
and Cherry laughed too.

Then Denise, Paul, and Theo noticed my fake beard and my too-tight suit.

"Damn, boss," Denise said, looking me up and down. "Looking good. The fake beard has it *all* going on."

"Eyes off, Virgin Mary," Malachi said. He pointed to his vest. "The position of Santa's favourite ho has been filled, thank you. If there will be one miraculous conception this year—"

I cut him off. "Okay, they don't need to hear that."

"I'm a donkey's arse," Theo said for no apparent reason. He smiled, his usual happy self. "We were going to be the three wise men, but this was funnier."

Malachi was watching Paul. "So," he hedged. "I seem to remember inventorying a riding crop not so long ago. I think it's in aisle R-S."

Paul spoke around the bit in his mouth. "I have one, thanks."

Malachi nodded slowly. "I'm oddly not surprised by this."

Paul neighed like a horse and Malachi laughed, and they walked off to the breakroom. The Virgin Mary and the arse of her donkey followed, and I looked to Cherry for some kind of answer but she just shrugged one bonbon shoulder.

"Coffee?" I asked.

"Yep." We joined the others in the breakroom for our morning coffee, but Denise was called to the back loading dock, and soon enough, the Virgin Mary was driving the forklift with her blue dress hitched up to reveal her work boots underneath.

Even for Christmas Eve, the work never stopped. Cage trolley after cage trolley needed processing. I would certainly be happy when the Christmas madness was over for another year.

One thing about being so busy was that it made time fly.

Malachi revealed the plate of red and green cupcakes for morning tea, and we exchanged our Kris Kringle gifts at lunchtime.

It was a staff gift exchange with a five-dollar limit, which meant gifts were usually funny, and shopping at the dollar shop or a thrift store was recommended. I got a very small cactus, which would look great on the kitchen window sill, and Malachi received a unicorn tape dispenser. He absolutely loved it.

The other gifts were a coffee cup with stuff for hot chocolate that Denise loved, a mason jar of Christmas mints that Theo was very happy with, Paul was stoked with the retro alarm clock that Malachi had found at a thrift store, and Cherry was chuffed with her novelty fluffy reindeer socks.

But we got back to the never-ending supply of misla-belled and lost mail, and I'd lost track of time when Paul found me down the bottom of aisle M-N watching Denise on the aerial platform retrieve a box from the top shelf for me.

"Hey," Paul whispered. "It's almost four thirty. Am I right to use your office to make the phone call or do you want me to sit out on the back dock?"

Shit.

"Oh, god," I mumbled, checking my watch. It was almost finishing time. "Uh . . ." Given we were closer to the loading dock than the office . . . "Where is he?"

"At his desk," Paul replied.

"The loading dock, then."

Paul nodded, took out his mobile phone, and walked out

through the loading area. "Ah, yeah, hi," he said, his voice perfectly different, higher but more scratchy.

How did he do that?

"What did you say your name was, sorry?" . . . "Oh, thanks, Malachi. Yeah, I sent something in the mail and it hasn't arrived. I was hoping you could tell me if it turned up there?"

Too nervous to keep listening, I pushed my cart back up the aisle.

This was the final piece. Well, tomorrow's Christmas gift was the final piece, but this was the last one that involved anyone else.

I made my way up to where I could hear Malachi on the phone. He was taking down the fake details that Paul was feeding him before he promised to call him back soon.

Malachi got up, frowning at the slip of paper in his hand, but walked to the far side of the warehouse to the old wooden file of catalogued cards. He always said they belonged in a 1950s library. Actually, he said they belonged in the library of Alexandria, by which he meant burned a long time ago.

Yes, we'd been digitalised for a long time, but the old catalogue cards were kept. The archive records were still valid, though rarely ever used, which was why I'd chosen them and probably explained Malachi's frown.

Paul had to give him a reference number, which would take Malachi a little time to find. I watched him, holding a parcel in my hand in case he looked my way so I could pretend to be busy. He double-checked the reference number, found the catalogue drawer, and began filing through the yellowed cards for what felt like forever. Eventually he pulled out one card, his frown deepening.

Staring at the card and without a glance in my direction,

he turned and walked down through a far aisle. He scanned the rows of parcels and letters, looking up to the highest rows, and he sighed.

"Denise?" he called out, going in search of her.

By the time she moved the aerial platform around to his aisle, we were running out of time. It was already a quarter to five.

But Denise found him the right storage box and handed it over, just like she was supposed to. He put the box on the ground and opened it, taking out various contents and scanning them, finding the one he was after.

"That doesn't make sense," he mumbled.

"What doesn't make sense?" I asked, feigning ignorance. I pulled my cart to a stop. "What have you got?"

"A guy called saying a parcel never arrived. He couldn't remember exactly when it was sent, but it was an older reference number. It should have been processed out of the system a long time ago."

He was still holding the smaller box. It was a square box, maybe five inches across. I nodded to it. "What's in it?"

"The inventory information was vague and incomplete. Who filled this out? Was this when Glenda was still here?"

I tried not to smile. "Open it."

He opened the box and pulled out a clear Christmas tree ornament. It was a clear globe filled with strips of paper.

But not just any paper . . .

Malachi gasped, his eyes going wide. "This is the same . . . it can't be . . ."

He took off up the aisle toward his desk. Denise waited until he was gone. "Well, it's in the hands of the gods now."

I felt a strange wave of relief. A calmness, a sense of well-being that all the wheels were in motion. Tomorrow morning, Christmas morning, would be the last piece of the puzzle.

If we made it that long.

"Ahhh!" Malachi yelled from his desk. It was loud enough to scare the pigeons off the roof. "It's the same!"

I smiled at Denise and she grinned right back at me. "He's going to drive you crazy tonight about this."

"I've got Moni on it. We're having dinner at her place because I knew we'd need the distraction." I sighed. "I better go act like I don't know what he's talking about."

"Give me your keys," she said, holding her hand out. "I'll put the box in the boot of your car, and I'll leave the key on your desk."

I handed the keys over. "Thank you."

I turned and found Malachi with his desk phone pressed to his ear. "It's not connected," he said. "His number's not connected. How can it not be connected? Did he give me the wrong number? Did they cut his phone off in the last twenty minutes? Julian, the number he gave me is wrong. I have no way of contacting him, oh my god—"

I put my hand on his shoulder. "Okay, the first thing you're going to do is breathe."

He breathed.

I took the phone from him and placed it back in the cradle. "Second thing, are you sure the number you wrote down is correct?"

The look he gave me told me, in no uncertain terms, that I should have known better than to have asked that.

"Sorry. Are you sure all these items are connected?"

He picked up the bauble ornament as though it was as precious as the Third Imperial Faberge egg. "Look at the paper," he said.

And sure enough, inside the bauble were strips of the

very same expensive paper with *Merry Christmas, My Love* written on every strand.

How could I see that much detail? I couldn't. Not exactly.

So how did I know what was written on the paper?

Because I wrote it.

There was something else in there, fixed to the bottom, which he couldn't see.

"It looks the same," I said.

Malachi rolled his eyes. "Of course it's the same."

"Didn't you say this was inventoried four years ago?"

He nodded. "It makes no sense." He picked up the first letter and its envelope. "Unless all of them are from four years ago and were just lost somehow . . ."

"Maybe," I offered.

"Sorry to interrupt," Theo said. "But it's five o'clock. Time to go. You have a great day tomorrow and I'll see you on Boxing Day."

"Same to you," I said.

He took his Kris Kringle gift and waved to the others as he left, still wearing the bottom half of the donkey outfit.

"Me too," Paul said. His smile was wide, but Malachi was too distracted to think anything of it. "Have a great Christmas."

"You too," I said. "Did you get your bridle and alarm clock?" Because that was a totally normal thing to ask.

He grinned and patted his satchel. "Sure did."

"Have a great day tomorrow," Malachi offered quietly.

He was obviously a little down. "Hey," I said, rubbing his arm. "We can't be late to Moni's tonight. Unless you fancy getting yelled at, because I certainly don't. How about you pack all this up and we can deal with it on Boxing Day."

The truth was, even if he could find the sender or the recipient and he put it back in the mail system, they weren't going to get it before Christmas.

He sighed and sagged, utterly defeated. "Ugh."

But he packed it all up, scanned the items, and inventoried them properly, and closed the lid on the box. He picked it up and with perfect timing, Denise pushed a trolley out. "Here, these are yours," she said gruffly. "I'll file that one. You need to put these away." She took the box he was holding and left the trolley with him. He wouldn't argue with Denise, and even if he was game enough, she'd already disappeared down the aisle.

Malachi groaned. "Come on, I'll help," I said, pushing the cart to the end of the first aisle.

"I'll help too," Cherry said, pulling Malachi by the elbow.

Between the three of us, it took all of ten minutes, but it was enough time for Denise to hide the box in the boot of my car and return my keys to my desk.

"Merry Christmas," Denise called out. "Loading dock is all locked up."

"Thank you. And Merry Christmas," I called back.

Cherry gave Malachi a hug as we were leaving. "Merry Christmas," she said. "Hope Santa's good to you."

"He better be," Malachi replied, still sullen.

"Merry Christmas, Cherry," I said, opening Malachi's car door. "Would Santa's favourite ho get in the car?"

That at least earned me a smile from Malachi. Cherry gave me a thumbs-up as she walked off.

I climbed in behind the wheel and took his hand. "Cheer up, baby. It's Christmas."

He let his head fall back on the headrest. "Hmm."

"Would you cheer up if I gave you one of your Christmas presents early?"

He sparked up at that. "Really?"

"After dinner, before bed," I said. "And not the main gift. That has to wait until Santa comes."

"Oh, believe me," he said, smiling now. "My sexy Santa's gonna come tonight."

CHAPTER SIX

THANK god Moni had been in on the whole secret. She'd listened to Malachi rant about the letters, the card, the ornament globe, how there were no clues, how none of it made sense.

She could have been a contender for an Oscar. She was wide-eyed, gasped in all the right places, acted concerned, perfectly confused about all the developments as he was, and gently changed the subject and distracted him so he never brought it up for the rest of the night.

We got home late, and I needed to bring in the box that was still in the boot without Malachi finding out. And there really was only one way to ensure he'd sleep so soundly, and that was to wear him out and leave him a boneless, sated heap on the bed.

It was hardly a chore.

Being inside him, making him moan and beg, was heaven to me. Taking him to that place where he was incoherent with pleasure, wringing his body of every ounce of bliss, having him cling to me, and the way he'd whisper my name, it felt like the reason I was put on this earth.

After he'd had enough, I took him to the shower and cleaned him up, then took him back to bed. I kissed the back of his head. "I'll just check on Mr Bojangles," I whispered. "Won't be long."

His only response was a sleepy snore.

I went downstairs, dashed out to the car, and brought the box back inside. I put it in a huge gift bag and slipped it behind the Christmas tree then put his final Christmas gift —the one I'd hidden at my parents—on the tree, nestled in with the tinsel and Malachi's artfully arranged decorations.

This was it.

Tomorrow morning, I'd be asking him to marry me.

I let out a deep breath and couldn't help but smile as I went back upstairs. I climbed into bed beside him and he sat up. "I was supposed to open a present tonight," he mumbled, his hair a beautiful mess.

I laughed and pulled him back into my arms. "Go to sleep, my love. Otherwise Santa won't come."

Malachi snuggled into me. "He already did. The proof is in my arse."

I snorted. Christ. "Night, Malachi."

"Night, Santa."

I WOKE up to a light tapping on my cheekbone. "Wake up, handsome. I made you coffee."

I stretched and opened my eyes. Malachi grinned at me. "Merry Christmas," he said, handing me a steaming cup.

I sat up and took the coffee. "Thank you. What time is it?"

"After eight. I want to cook you breakfast," he said.

It was normally me who looked after him. "Merry Christmas to me."

He grinned. "Come on. Then we can do presents. We need to be at your folks by eleven and you need to make that salad dressing. We're busy, busy today."

"Breakfast first. What are you making me?"

"Eggs and bacon and grilled tomato with toast." He skipped happily down the stairs. "Come on, sleepyhead."

Smiling, I took my coffee and followed him down to the kitchen. He had his head in the fridge and turned around, his hands full of eggs and bacon, took one look at me, and stopped. "Oh."

I looked down at myself. I was shirtless, wearing only the soft sleep pants he'd bought me for my birthday. "What?" I asked. "I slept beside you all night wearing these."

"Oh, I just like . . . damn, you look so hot in those. I can see your cock just hanging at half-mast. Should I salute? Or just drop to my knees and open my mouth? What's half-mast protocol?"

I rolled my eyes and sat on the stool at the breakfast bar. If we started something now, we'd be late to my parents'. "You can make me breakfast. This coffee is good, by the way."

He smiled proudly. "Thank you."

"Want me to do anything?"

"Not yet."

He busied himself scrambling eggs, frying bacon, and grilling tomato. I made us more coffee, popped the bread into the toaster, and we ate breakfast at the table. He'd put a centrepiece of eucalypt, gold gumnuts, and red bottlebrush on the table; we used the Christmas serviettes and placemats.

And as we ate, I couldn't help but smile. I was about to ask him to marry me. He had no idea what was coming, but he was so happy on this Christmas morning, and I'd never loved him more.

"What are you smiling at me like that for?" he asked.

I put my fork down. "There is simply no measure for how much I love you," I said.

He paused as if my words had touched him physically. "Oh. I love you too."

"Are you done with breakfast? I want to give you your presents."

"I should clean up the kitchen first. I made a bit of a mess."

It was true. He had. But that could wait. I stood up and held out my hand. "I'll do that later. Presents first."

He was obviously a little confused but happy to oblige. He slid his hand into mine. "Okay."

I led him to the couch beside the tree and had him sit. "Yours first."

He pointed to the pile of red and gold wrapped items. "Yours have the gold bows. Your family's have the red bows, and my family have ribbon. I thought it was best if I used a visual method. They have tags of course, but it was easier . . ."

I handed him his first gift. It was a pair of the linen pants he'd wanted. He saw them in a shop and said he wanted them so he'd know what it was like to walk on some Italian beach at sunset or whatever. The second was the super expensive silk pillowcases he wanted. He'd read on some beauty thing that they were better for your complexion but had cried when he saw the price.

"Oh my god, you've spoiled me," he said, holding the silk to his face.

"There's one more," I said, taking the envelope hidden in the tree and handing it to him.

"Dearest Malachi Keogh," he whispered, reading the front of the envelope. "This paper . . ."

While he was opening it, I took the box from behind the tree and put it at his feet.

He held up the slip of paper. He was confused, worried even. "It says 'This Christmas, I wish you the gift of warmth and peace in knowing how much you are loved'."

Then he looked up at me. "This is the same paper, the same writing as the letters we got at work."

I smiled. "Read the back."

He flipped it over. "'Open the ornament'." He shot me a wild look. "What ornament?"

I took the lid off the box at his feet and carefully lifted out the smaller box with the ornament in it, and I gave it to him.

"This ornament," I said.

His eyes became glassy as he took it out, looking closely at what was inside the clear globe. "It has little bits of paper in it, with writing . . . Julian . . ." He swallowed hard.

"Open it."

He turned it over in his hand. "It doesn't open."

"Yes, it does."

He stared at me, teary, and shook his head. But he inspected the ornament and gently twisted it to reveal two halves. A pile of the handwritten slips fell onto his lap and he began to cry. He could see now that the type of paper, the fancy writing, was all the same. "This was you?"

I nodded. "Look inside it."

He wiped a tear away with the back of his hand and lifted out the remaining slips of paper to reveal the one small paper box that was stuck to the bottom. It was about an inch wide. About big enough to hold a ring.

He knew. His eyes went wide, and tears spilled down onto his cheeks. "Oh god."

"Open it," I whispered.

His fingers shook but he peeled it out of the ornament and popped the little paper pouch open. "Julian," he sobbed.

I went to the floor in front of him, on both knees, and took his hand. "I want you to know how much you are loved. And I would be honoured to be called your husband, from this day until forever. Malachi Keogh, will you marry me?"

A flood of tears burst free, and he nodded and sobbed. "Yes."

I pulled him into a hug and he cried into my neck. "You did all this for me. All the letters at work, the cards, all of it?"

"Of course I did. The paper, the writing. And everyone at work helped. Even my mum and Moni. They were all part of it."

He pulled back, wiping at his face. "You really want to marry me?"

"More than anything in this world."

His chin wobbled. "I love you so much."

"Want to put the ring on?"

"Yes!" he fumbled with the small paper pouch but let the ring slide out onto his palm. It was matt black but the inside was bright purple, and of course, he started to cry again. "It's perfect."

"I wanted something to reflect you," I said, taking the ring, and holding his left hand, I slid it onto his ring finger.

He threw his arms around my neck and hugged me

fiercely. "I can't wait to marry you," he said. Then he pulled back and met my gaze. "And the calligraphy? Since when can you write like that?"

"I used to do calligraphy back in high school. It took some practice. But the paper," I explained, "I had it delivered from Japan. I wanted it to be special, and something you could keep forever. The Dearest Milton James letters were so perfect, I wanted to show you that my love for you was forever. Like theirs was. I don't know . . ."

He took my face in his hands. "The tips of your ears are pink. It means you're nervous. Don't be nervous. The paper is perfect. Julian, I love it. I love all of it."

"I thought we could frame the Christmas card, if you want," I suggested. "With the kirigami and the origami trees and reindeer. It was actually really expensive, and maybe if we frame it, we can bring it out every Christmas like a tradition or something."

He got teary again. "Our first tradition. In our little family. Oh my god." He wiped his tears away. "I want to frame them all." Then he straightened, having obviously just remembered something. "Oh shit. Your present. Let me get it for you."

He shot up off the couch and picked up a red wrapped box. He handed it to me but then stopped, looking at the ring on his finger. He grinned at me. "Look!"

I laughed and got up onto the couch and took the gift. It was expertly wrapped like he always did. Inside was a folder from a travel agent. "Malachi," I whispered.

"I spoke to Dad and got time off approved for both of us," he said quickly. "It's two weeks in Thailand. A resort with a tropical beach. Please don't be mad. It's booked for July. When it's quieter at work and freezing cold here. And you haven't had a proper holiday in forever, and Dad said he can get staff from the night shift to fill in. Please don't be mad."

I shook my head. "I'm not mad at all. This is . . . very generous. Malachi, this must have cost a fortune."

"It did. But it's kind of a birthday present for both of us as well and—"

"And we should use it as a honeymoon."

He stared. "What?"

"We should get married. In July."

"This July?" His eyes were wide. "Like seven months from now?"

I nodded. "I would marry you today if I could. Right now, even."

Malachi suddenly looked panicked. "Julian, how can I plan a whole wedding in less than seven months?"

"Baby, if anyone can do it, you can."

"Um . . ." He shook his head and studied the ring on his finger for a second. "Okay. Let's do it. I don't care if we get married at the mail centre."

"We're not getting married at work."

He smirked. "Well, no. But we'll make it happen. Somewhere. It doesn't matter. At the end of the day, the wedding doesn't matter. It's the marriage that matters."

I smiled and kissed him. "I love you, Malachi Keogh."

He gasped. "Names. What are we doing with names? I could be Malachi Keogh-Pollard. With a fancy hyphen and everything." He stood up quickly. "I need to practice my new signature."

I laughed. Keogh-Pollard sounded good to me. "Dearest Malachi Keogh-Pollard," I said.

He came out of the kitchen with a pen and a huge grin. "Yes?"

"Does Julian Keogh-Pollard have a nice ring to it?"

He nodded, getting teary again. "Yes! Dearest Julian Keogh-Pollard." He threw himself at me and I wrapped my arms around him so easily.

I kissed the side of his head. "Merry Christmas, Malachi Keogh."

"It's Malachi Keogh-Pollard."

"Well, not yet."

He pulled back, his eyes huge and imploring. "Excuse me, please don't rain on my Christmas parade."

I kissed him. "Merry Christmas, Malachi Keogh-Pollard."

He grinned. "That's better. Thank you, Julian Keogh-Pollard."

"You should probably call everyone we know and tell them you said yes. They'll be waiting to hear."

"Everyone? Everyone knew about this before me?"

"Pretty much."

He pouted, then waved his hand at the dining table. "You should probably clean up after breakfast. And then you should probably fuck me stupid until we need to leave for your parents for lunch."

I laughed. "Is that right?"

He nodded with an adorable smile. "Yep." He put his hand to his chest and winked. "I'm your Christmas ho ho ho, remember?"

He found his phone and called Moni first, and I smiled at his excited shriek and the string of curses he called her for keeping such a secret from him as I cleared the table.

Would I ever get sick of him bossing me around? Of him being loud and excitable, a ball of energy, or insatiable in the bedroom?

Absolutely not.

I was about to sign up for a lifetime of it, and it still

wouldn't be enough. Not now, not ever. He was going to marry me, gift me with a promise of forever.

I would want for nothing more.

MERRY CHRISTMAS TO US.

The End

ABOUT THE AUTHOR

N.R. Walker is an Australian author, who loves her genre of gay romance. She loves writing and spends far too much time doing it, but wouldn't have it any other way.

She is many things: a mother, a wife, a sister, a writer. She has pretty, pretty boys who live in her head, who don't let her sleep at night unless she gives them life with words.

She likes it when they do dirty, dirty things... but likes it even more when they fall in love.

She used to think having people in her head talking to her was weird, until one day she happened across other writers who told her it was normal.

She's been writing ever since...

ALSO BY N.R. WALKER

Titles in Audio:

Pieces of Us

Tic-Tac-Mistletoe

Lacuna

Bossy

Code Red

Free Reads:

Sixty Five Hours

Learning to Feel

His Grandfather's Watch (And The Story of Billy and Hale)

The Twelfth of Never (Blind Faith 3.5)

Twelve Days of Christmas (Sixty Five Hours Christmas)

Best of Both Worlds

Translated Titles:

Italian

Fiducia Cieca (Blind Faith)

Attraverso Questi Occhi (Through These Eyes)

Preso alla Sprovvista (Blindside)

Il giorno del Mai (Blind Faith 3.5)

Cuore di Terra Rossa Serie (Red Dirt Heart Series)

Natale di terra rossa (Red dirt Christmas)

Intervento di Retrofit (Elements of Retrofit)

A Chiare Linee (Clarity of Lines)

Senso D'appartenenza (Sense of Place)

Spencer Cohen Serie (including Yanni's Story)

Punto di non Ritorno (Point of No Return)

Punto di Rottura (Breaking Point)

Punto di Partenza (Starting Point)

Imago (Imago)

Il desiderio di un soldato (A Soldier's Wish)

Scambiato (Switched)

Galassie e Oceani (Galaxies and Oceans)

French

Confiance Aveugle (Blind Faith)

A travers ces yeux: Confiance Aveugle 2 (Through These Eyes)

Aveugle: Confiance Aveugle 3 (Blindside)

À Jamais (Blind Faith 3.5)

Cronin's Key Series

Au Coeur de Sutton Station (Red Dirt Heart)

Partir ou rester (Red Dirt Heart 2)

Faire Face (Red Dirt Heart 3)

Trouver sa Place (Red Dirt Heart 4)

Le Poids de Sentiments (The Weight of It All)

Un Noël à la sauce Henry (A Very Henry Christmas)

Une vie à Refaire (Switched)

Evolution (Evolved)

Galaxies & Océans

German

Flammende Erde (Red Dirt Heart)

Lodernde Erde (Red Dirt Heart 2)

Sengende Erde (Red Dirt Heart 3)

Ungezähmte Erde (Red Dirt Heart 4)

Vier Pfoten und ein bisschen Zufall (Finders Keepers)

Ein Kleines bisschen Versuchung (The Weight of It All)

Ein Kleines Bisschen Fur Immer (A Very Henry Christmas)

Weil Leibe uns immer Bliebt (Switched)

Drei Herzen eine Leibe (Three's Company)

Über uns die Sterne, zwischen uns die Liebe (Galaxies and Oceans)

Unnahbares Herz (Blind Faith 1)

Sehendes Herz (Blind Faith 2)

Thai

Sixty Five Hours (Thai translation)

Finders Keepers (Thai translation)

Spanish

Sesenta y Cinco Horas (Sixty Five Hours)

Código Rojo (Code Red)

Chinese

Blind Faith